Melissa Mouse
Moves House

This book belongs to

....

....

Text and compilation Copyright © 1994 Michelle Lovric
Illustrations Copyright © 1994 Royle Publications Ltd

This edition published by Longmeadow Press
201 High Ridge Road, Stamford, Connecticut 06904

Design and Color Reproduction by Camway Autographics.
Set in Utopia

Library of Congress Cataloging-in-Publication Data
ISBN 0 - 681 - 45441 - 5
First Longmeadow Press Edition
0 9 8 7 6 5 4 3 2 1

Royle

Produced by Royle Publications Ltd, Royle House, Wenlock Road, London N1 7ST, England.
Created by Michelle Lovric, 53 Shelton Street, Covent Garden, London WC2H 9HE, England.
Printed and bound in Singapore

Melissa Mouse

Moves House

illustrated by Gillian Roberts
story by Michelle Lovric

LONGMEADOW
PRESS

Melissa Mouse was sleepy
all the time.

There were
loud sounds
at her house
all the time,

but Melissa Mouse still slept.

First, there were her
eleven baby brothers.

Then there were twelve!
They made *a lot* of noise.

And then there were her fourteen -

No, Fifteen! -

Baby sisters.

Her sisters made a lot of noise, too.

It was always someone's
birthday in their house!

It seemed to be
noisy all the time,

but it was hard to wake Melissa Mouse.

The only thing that kept Melissa Mouse awake
was playing with her special friend, Sam.

Her eyes were wide open and sparkling
when Sam was there.

Day and
night,
Melissa
and Sam
had fun.

The best thing
about Sam was
that he liked
to nap almost
as much as
Melissa Mouse

Eventually the mouse family grew so big that they could not fit round the table. When it was someone's birthday, Father and Mother Mouse had to make a picnic outside in the garden.

"It's time to move to a bigger house"
said Father Mouse.

Their friends across the street were sad to
see them leaving.

Mother Mouse washed the windows one last time and packed one last picnic.

Then they were ready to move to their new home.

All the little mice helped to carry books, bottles and furniture to their new home.

Melissa Mouse helped, too.
She was not sleeping that day!

At the new house there was lots of room and it was a lot quieter.

But now Melissa Mouse **couldn't** sleep.
She wrote lots of letters to Sam.
"I miss you" she wrote.

Melissa Mouse was
never sleepy now.

She wrote

and wrote

and wrote.

One day she wrote a
story about Sam.
Mother Mouse thought it
was very good and sent it
to the newspaper.

After writing so hard for so long,
Melissa Mouse needed to take a little nap.

19

The next day a letter came for Melissa Mouse. She had won first prize in a story contest.

First prize was a key to her very own house.

So Melissa Mouse
and Sam were married.

Her brothers and sisters came to
the wedding and made *a lot* of noise.

"Good night!" said Melissa Mouse.
"This has been a wonderful day".
But Sam didn't answer her
because he was already fast asleep.

The end.